NICK AND THE GENIE

BRIAN MORSE

Nick
and the Genie

Illustrated by Deborah Meadows

LUTTERWORTH PRESS
Cambridge

Lutterworth Press
7 All Saints' Passage
Cambridge CB2 3LS

British Library Cataloguing in Publication Data
Morse, Brian
Nick and the genie. — (Fantasia).
I. Title
823′   914 [J]   PZ7
ISBN 0-7188-2688-4

First published 1987 by Lutterworth Press

Printed in Great Britain by
Redwood Burn Limited, Trowbridge, Wiltshire.

For Lisa

1

The applause died away, the children began to file out of the school hall with many a backward glance. When the last echo of a footstep had faded in the corridor Amos said quietly to the genie who had been taking the bow beside him, "Right, Mecca, time to pack away. And let's make it quick, shall we? We've a three hundred mile journey. We've been on the road two weeks, and I want to sleep in my own bed tonight."

"I feel weary too, O Amos. I also have been on the road a fortnight," the genie grumbled, changing from a splendidly robed prince into a purple cloud which hovered irritably around Amos' head. "Also, is it not about time Shybad pulled his weight? And as for Nushing, genie of the lamp, the last time I saw her lift a finger — "

"You genies!" Amos interrupted. "Why are you always arguing? Shybad! Yes, Shybad! I can see you hiding! That trick doesn't fool me any longer." A sulky red cloud appeared from behind a row of chairs on the far side of the hall. "Shybad, you and Mecca get everything packed away. In the meantime I'll collect our fee from the headmaster and see whether he wants to book us for our Christmas tour. And as for Nushing, what she carried was the show. She deserves a rest."

As he drew back the doors at the end of the hall Amos heard Mecca muttering again. Genies! He pulled the door to behind him with an angry tug. Thank goodness we're going home. I can't stand much more of their arguing. Genies! If only I'd gone in for a more sensible job!

That evening, about seven, nearly half-way home, the engine of the Amos Entertainments van began to make a fearful noise. Amos pulled into a convenient lay-by. As the occasional car went past he fastened up the bonnet and peered inside. Oil was oozing from the engine onto the gravel and tarmac. Amos had no idea what was wrong. He got his coat and walked up the road to the telephone box he'd seen about half a mile back.

"R.A.C.? I've got a problem."

Amos had another problem. His R.A.C. membership was out of date. They wouldn't come.

Back at the van again he sighed deeply, then opened up the rear doors. He looked at the three straw-filled boxes. Which genie? Not Nushing in her oriental lamp. She'd already worked hard enough. It would have to be Shybad or Mecca, one of that sulky pair. He seized Mecca's bottle and pulled the cork. Mecca was usually more reasonable than Shybad.

"Yes, Master?" The green cloud eyed him blearily. "Is it tomorrow already? Are we home? I could sleep for a hundred years."

"And so you shall," Amos said. "Or at least for a

hundred hours," he added hastily for the genies never forgot a promise. "But only after we've got this van going again. Come and listen to the engine."

"Well?" he asked anxiously after the genie had floated backwards and forwards, in and out of the engine compartment for a minute or more.

"I would say your big end has gone," Mecca told him gloomily. "May I go back to sleep again?"

"Big end?" Amos was horrified. "That sounds awful. How long does it take to fix a big end?"

"Three hours. You will need a block and tackle to lift the engine. Do not omit to remember that."

"With a van-load of sleeping genies! You must be joking if you think I'm going to call a garage — or that I have the money to spend," Amos said indignantly.

"We were born when no one had even dreamt of the motor car," Mecca said. "Master, may I go back to sleep? Call Shybad if you require any help. This mucky work is more in his line. Good night, Amos, dearest Master."

"A big end for my van is what I need and a big end I will have," Amos said stubbornly. "Fetch me one! Now! After that, sleep! A hundred hours! I promise."

"But, Master, I must trace the design, dig the iron, refine the steel, mould the part. This is no second-class engine you have here, but a high-quality job, made of the finest steel. Did not the second-hand car salesman who practically gave it away to you say so? This is no five second job. Make Shybad do it, I implore you. He has done practically nothing today, nothing!"

"You make the big end, Shybad will fit it. Then you

can both sleep. Now go wherever it is you go and make it! Be as quick as you can!" Amos commanded.

It was dark, however, before Mecca returned protesting, "It is no easy thing, Master, to make this stupidly named object. Big end! A thousand years ago we did not have such names." By the time Shybad had finished fitting it the night was even darker.

Amos trudged back up to the phone box and called his wife.

"We'll have to sleep in the lay-by," he told her. "I haven't enough petrol to get to the nearest filling station that's open at this time of night. Yes, I sent Shybad to check. In any case I've lost almost all the oil out of the engine. The genies claim the special oil I need is almost impossible for them to make. I'm too tired to argue. See you tomorrow, barring accidents. Good night, love."

As he reached the van Amos could hear Shybad and Mecca bickering. He banged on the van's rear doors. "Shut it, you two!" he shouted. They were arguing about Nushing. Both claimed that the beautiful Nushing liked him best. Contrary beasts, he thought.

It rained during the night, battering on the van's steel roof. But Amos was woken before that by yet another violent argument coming from the back.

He opened his eyes. He had stretched out as far as he could across the two front seats. He listened to the high-pitched voices the genies used to shout to each other from their bottles. They spoke in ancient Persian. Amos had tried to learn it once but it was too difficult, so now he could not understand what they

4

were saying. He knew, though, that it was insulting.

However did I get into genies? he wondered for the thousandth time. He sighed. Silly creatures. They don't really mean each other or anyone else harm. Actually they're as soft as they come, quite tender-hearted. Why didn't I take up something ordinary for a career? He tried to think of something safe and simple and interesting. As usual he drew a blank.

The argument and the din the genies were making got worse. Amos climbed out and opened the van's back doors. He shivered. Tall clouds were banking up in the west.

"You two!" he shouted. "You've been asking to sleep ever since we started on this trip. Now you're keeping me awake with your twitterings. Shut it!"

"O Master!" Shybad said. "It is beneath my dignity to sleep in the vicinity of such an idiot."

"Idiot yourself!" Mecca said. "Clod-hopping carpet-raveller!"

"Shut up, I said!" Amos shouted. "That is my last word!" He strode back round to the front of the van.

"Our master has forgotten to shut the van doors," Shybad remarked a few minutes later to Mecca.

"A blind ant could have observed that!" Mecca replied. The quarrel wasn't over as far as he was concerned, even if he'd long forgotten what it was about.

Shybad's bottle bounced with rage, and bounced and bounced. It bounced right out of the van.

Later in the night the rain came down in torrents. The lay-by filled up with water. The water came up to the van's axles and nearly floated it away. With many a gurgle it drained away into a nearby stream, taking the bottle and Shybad with it.

2

About half past ten next morning, not so very far from the lay-by, a boy called Nick was on his way to school. He was late because he'd been to the dentist. Nick took his time. He'd only been for a check-up but he meant to squeeze a little extra freedom out of the appointment. At last, however, he arrived at the end of the school drive.

A stream ran down from the right, under the end of the drive. It ran on through the school grounds. Nick stopped and looked down at it. He fancied taking his shoes and socks off and paddling. It was a warm sunny morning and the water was a little higher than usual, making it seem even more inviting. There had been a storm in the night, Mum had said. Dare he? He looked at the school, wondering, then suddenly at the stream again. What was it he could see in the water, caught against a stone? He climbed down onto the bank below. Nick peered cautiously. The stream was too wide to lean across without danger of falling in.

The mystery object was a largish bottle. He looked for a stick, found one, nudged the bottle over to his feet and picked it up. It was made of thick green glass which didn't let the light through, but Nick didn't think there was anything inside except a spot of liquid which seemed to swill about as he rocked it to and fro. There was no clue as to what had been in it once, no label or design on its side.

There didn't seem to be any reason not to extract the cork. Nick struggled with it briefly, then the cork popped out.

A moment later he wished he'd left the bottle well alone.

Amos had woken late in the lay-by. Seeing the time on his watch, he immediately scrambled behind the wheel, started the engine and drove straight off.

At the petrol station — the green oil warning light had been flashing at him all the way — he noticed first the unfastened back doors, then that Shybad's bottle was missing.

Amos felt very angry as he pulled up in the lay-by again. Trust this to happen. Wasn't he already late enough? He wasn't too worried though. Genies might have the strength to jerk their bottles about a little, but that was all. The bottle would be just where they'd parked last night. Amos went to pick it up.

There was a nasty patch of oil where they'd been, but no bottle. By now all the flood water had dried up in the sun, so Amos knew nothing about that. He stood and scratched his head in puzzlement. Where could Shybad have gone? Then a dreadful thought struck him. Had someone stopped in the lay-by and picked up the bottle? Worse still, had they opened it? A genie in a temper needed very careful handling, very careful indeed. And he had promised Mecca he could sleep for a hundred hours. He'd certainly be in a foul mood if he was woken up.

Not far away, down the stream, a little red cloud rose from the neck of the bottle. Nick hastily threw the bottle down by the edge of the water. The red cloud convulsed, grew, and began to take on a shape. It grew taller than Nick himself. A head, then a body, formed out of the cloud and the creature stood in the air above the stream.

The face grew burning eyes, came down to Nick's level and glared at him. If looks could kill! The creature had grown a mouth and nose. It was thick-lipped and wore an incredibly stupid expression. Worst of all, it seemed extremely annoyed.

Nick took a step backwards towards the bank he'd just come down.

"You're not edging off like that!" the creature screeched. "Not after uncorking me. How dare you!"

"I didn't know you were inside," Nick said, unable to take his eyes away.

"What else did you expect to be inside this bottle? Sardines?"

"I'm afraid I've never seen your kind of bottle before," Nick whispered.

"Well, of course you haven't! But don't they tell you the stories about genies?"

"I thought they weren't true."

"Not true! Genies not true! How dare you!"

"I'd have thought you'd be glad to get out of the bottle," Nick said. It was a little bold, but he wanted to change the subject. It was a mistake.

"Glad! That was the first decent sleep I'd had all night! All week! All month! Next you'll be asking for three wishes, commanding and ordering me to do this and that!" The genie swayed backwards and forwards. It was getting terribly worked up. Nick could see how its body narrowed to a wispy tail which trailed back into the bottle.

"Three wishes?" he said, suddenly interested. "I'd forgotten about them."

"No, you haven't got three wishes," the genie screamed. "Not one or a million! I'm going to do the commanding around here! I, Shybad! I'm fed up with being told to do this or do that! I bounced around all night till that stone trapped me. Stupid stream! You want to try being shut in a bottle that is bobbing around in a stream! Now goodbye and good riddance!" The genie began to shrink.

"No! Stop!" Nick shouted. He felt obstinate. All genie stories agreed on one thing, and that was that genies granted you three wishes.

"What do you mean — stop?" The genie stopped shrinking and regarded Nick with a baleful eye. "Give me one good reason why I should do any such thing."

"You owe me three wishes."

"And what if I do?" the genie sneered.

"You're going to give them to me."

"Am I?"

Nick and the genie stared at each other, but however

burning its eyes were it was the genie who looked away first.

"Yes! You are!" Nick said triumphantly.

"Truly I am," the genie said. It had a sly look on its face which Nick didn't notice in his excitement. "And what might that first wish be, O Master?" The tone of its voice should have warned him too.

"First . . . first . . ." Nick didn't know what to choose.

"Yes, O Master? I don't like to rush you, but we genies do have our own lives to lead."

"Oh! I know!" Nick was suddenly inspired. "Shrink me."

"Shrink you?" the genie said.

"Yes! The way you do yourself!"

"Any particular size, O Master?" the genie said. Its sly look got worse.

Nick gestured with his hands. "Oh — about like this. No, smaller than that. Yes, like this." He indicated a height about the length of one of the rulers you get in pencil cases.

Nick shrank till he was less than half the height of the bottle. Shrinking didn't hurt, though when he looked down the ground seemed to be coming up to hit him. Nick put a hand up to steady himself. It slid down the neck of the bottle.

The genie was now a gigantic red billowy cloud, like the side of a house. It bent down and boomed above his head, "Wish granted, O Master. Two wishes left. If you need me, contact me. That is, if you can!" With that it flowed at great speed back into the bottle. A thin red arm reappeared and grasped the cork. With a plop the mouth was sealed off.

Nick stood amazed by his surroundings. Grass stems were like the trunks of young trees. An insect crawling along waving its feelers, was the size of a cat. A butterfly flapped past him and its wings made a breeze. The sky seemed higher, the world larger. It was a glorious feeling.

Nick knew what he wanted to do now. To show his class, particularly Mark, his best friend, what had happened to him. But now the school was so far away. How was he to get there? Walk? That far! Then he thought of the genie. The genie could take him. As long as it didn't count as a second wish of course.

He knocked on the bottle and called, "Hey! I want you a moment, Shybad!" There was no answer. He knocked again and shouted. Still no answer. Suddenly it struck him what the genie had meant by "if you can". The spiteful creature!

He would have to uncork it again.

He put his arms round the middle of the bottle and began to rock it to and fro. It was like wrestling with a pillar-box. All of a sudden the bottle swayed. Nick jumped out of the way with a shout of triumph. The bottle hit the ground with a crash. Now for the cork.

However, there was something Nick hadn't given a thought to. The ground sloped. Instead of Nick being able to pull the cork out, the bottle pushed him out of the way. At first slowly, then with gathering speed, it rolled down the bank and into the stream. The water took it. With a swirl of current his other two wishes disappeared under the bridge.

13

3

In the lay-by Amos shook Mecca's bottle. It was no use. He peered down the neck but there was nothing to be seen. There never was if they didn't want, and Mecca had obviously decided to make himself scarce. "A very deep sleep" was how he'd explain it later. "I didn't hear a thing. A hundred thousand apologies, O Master, from the depths of my heart."

Amos thought, then picked up the lamp from the third box. He rubbed it. There was sleep in Nushing's eyes as she greeted him.

"Nushing, I have a serious problem. You know I wouldn't wake you otherwise."

Nushing smiled. No wonder Mecca and Shybad are half in love with her, Amos thought. This morning she was in the form of a princess. Bangles tinkled on her wrists. She wore a jewel-encrusted gown. No dowdy red or purple clouds for her.

"I've no idea where Shybad is, whether he's somewhere nearby or whether someone's picked him up," he finished lamely.

"This I will do for you," Nushing said. She yawned exquisitely. "Look out over the fields," she commanded, and yawned again. "There. Yes, there."

14

Nick hesitated for a full ten seconds on the edge of the stream. Then he turned and ran up the bank. The water was far too deep for him, the stream far too wide. However, he could cross the bridge and follow the stream and the bottle down towards the school. It shouldn't take him too long to catch it up.

Before he reached the top of the bank, however, the ground began to tremble. A terrible roaring sound filled the air. Nick dropped flat as an enormous bright red object hurtled over the bridge just above him. It sped down the drive, throwing out a storm of choking dust. Nick twisted round in terror. What on earth had that been? A fighter plane crash-landing? Was the school going to be razed to the ground? At the bottom of the drive, however, the headmaster was backing his Mini into its place. Was that all it had been? The head clambered out and strode up the school front steps.

There came more noise from the road, a scuffling and crunching. What now? Nick knelt down behind a head-high tuft of grass and peeped anxiously between the stalks. All this time the bottle was floating further and further away. I should never have trusted that creature, he thought. It had a tricky look about it. I should have made all my wishes at once, wealth, health, happiness, all the usual ones.

A group of children and grown ups was coming up the road. The little ones toddling along next to their mothers looked enormous. So did their dog. And how fast they moved!

A child of four who lived in the next road to Nick

began to run ahead of his mother, calling, "Mummy! A puppet! Look! A puppet!"

Nick knew exactly what that child was: a terror. He began to leap down the bank, remembering too late that it was a long distance for him now and much steeper for his tiny legs. He landed with such a bump he was nearly knocked out.

Nick picked himself up, slipped into the cold water and waded under the bridge, just as the child reached the spot where he had been a few seconds before.

Amos walked into the middle of the field next to the lay-by. He felt a real fool. There was a magpie hopping about by the far hedge. Amos called to it, just as Nushing had instructed him, using the exact sounds. His first attempt was none too successful. A sparrow dropped a piece of straw in his hair and promised to be back with more. At the corner of the field a cow — or was it a bull? — turned and began to trot in his direction. He tried again, and then again.

At last the magpie took notice. It hopped into the air and began to flap towards him. "Qwark?" it said inquiringly. "Qwark?"

Nick stood just inside the bridge. The water was over his knees and freezing cold.

The four year old reached the bottom of the bank. For a moment Nick thought he was going to follow him in the stream, but at the last moment the child drew back. He knelt and twisted his neck to look.

"Mummy!" he called. "I can see it! I can see it! Come and look!"

His mother, however, called him from the top of the bank. "Daniel! Come away! Come here at once! Do you hear me?"

"But, Mum," he cried. "I want it! I want the live puppet!"

"Daniel, come away from that water. It's deep. I'm not warning you again!"

"But, Mum — " There was the thud of heavy feet. Daniel leaped up hastily. "But, Mum — !" The sound of a smack was followed by a wail.

Serves him right, Nick thought.

"How many times have I told you not to play by water!" Daniel's mother shouted.

A few seconds later, however, the dog came jumping down too. It waded straight in.

Nick pressed back hard against the concrete and held his breath.

The dog, which was many times Nick's size, peered into the semi-darkness. It sniffed and began to paw the water in excitement. Nick was drenched. The dog ignored the voices calling it from the top of the bank. It took a step nearer Nick and peered again. It saw him.

In a panic Nick turned to run further on. Then he stopped. If the dog gave chase he'd be bowled over and crushed in the narrow space. He took a chance. He edged a little towards it and said gently, "Hey, boy!"

The dog's eyes showed surprise but its tail began to wag. Nick could almost hear it thinking, "People don't

17

usually come this size." Then a hand grabbed it by the collar and hauled it out of Nick's sight. A voice said, "Probably a cat. He's always after them." Another voice said, "More likely a rat down there." "Ugh!" several voices said. Nick shivered at the thought. Other voices boomed and laughed. Daniel shouted about "his puppet" again and cried. Then there was the sound of many feet tramping over the bridge.

If they're visiting the school they'll have to come back up the drive again, Nick reasoned to himself. So I'll have to stay put till they do. It's all open ground up to the school. How long will they be? There's no way of guessing. Where will the bottle have drifted to by then? Probably not very far for a normal-sized person, but for me? Even if I catch the bottle up, how am I going to get the cork out? Worry about that when it happens, Nick told himself. But whatever possessed me to make such a stupid wish?

Above his head Nick heard the rumble of the feet again. He gingerly made his way to the other end of the tunnel and peered out. He saw Daniel and his family making their way up the road. The coast was clear. He began to run along the bank after the bottle.

4

Nick ran for a little, but soon slowed down to a fast walk and then he just trudged. Being fifteen centimetres high was pretty exhausting in a full-size world.

At the point where the stream ran closest to the school building he slumped down beside a tree. The two hundred metres he'd covered had felt like miles and he still couldn't see the bottle.

Not far from Nick (if you were a normal size, that was) the headmaster was sorting through a pile of mail in his office. Nick could just see him through the window. As he watched, Mrs Bate, the school secretary, came in and asked him a question. The headmaster picked up the phone and dialled. He smiled and began to talk. A couple of minutes later he finished the phone call and started looking through his letters again.

Nick stood up and sighed. The water in the stream raced past him so quickly. Then it struck him. The stream curved here round the school's adventure playground. He could take a short-cut. He'd surprise that genie yet!

He toiled up the bank to the path that ran along beside the school. Now he was below the curtains of the staffroom, where Mrs Bate had her typewriter and filing cabinets. Nick just couldn't resist a quick peek. The window-sill was high above him, but with an enormous effort he pulled himself up and managed to peep over. Mrs Bate was battering away furiously at her machine. Nick held on as long as he could, enjoying for the first time the sensation of being really small and able to spy. This was why he'd made his wish. Now for his own classroom. He moved on.

Extra carefully, for there were no net curtains here, he pulled himself up again. Nearly everyone's eyes were on Mrs Wright, his teacher, who was speaking to the class, though two girls were secretly seeing to each other's hair and some friends of Nick's were playing a game under their desk. Mark was yawning into his hand. They were getting ready to write a story. Nick didn't mind missing that. It was too hot today for writing stories. He dropped to the ground, his arms aching from the effort of holding himself up.

Inside, Mrs Wright clapped her hands. Chairs began to scrape, children to stand up. Some trays were by the window. Nick ducked down as children began to crowd in his direction. Though he would have liked to have surprised them with his size, that would have to come later. The bottle and that crafty genie came first.

But why not? Why shouldn't he? He'd let them see him! What was the point of being small if no one knew about it?

Nick wasn't alone on the path. A bird had landed a couple of metres from him, a largish, glossy, black and white bird. Nick froze.

The bird hopped a couple of steps closer. Its jet-black eyes regarded him.

Nick raised his arms, took a step towards the bird and shouted. It backed off a little, but didn't fly away. It seemed utterly fascinated by him. It cocked its head on one side, then made a hop and jump forward. Nick stepped back and found himself jammed up against the wall. He looked around wildly. What did the stupid thing want?

Suddenly the outside door to the classroom crashed open. The bird hastily flew off across the adventure playground. Mrs Wright came out. Without letting go of the door she bent round to the other side of it and fastened it to the wall. Back into the classroom she went, calling, "Quiet now and settle down, James! Stop that! And Joanne, leave Julie alone! Debbie, young lady, young ladies are not supposed to do that! Back to your tables with your books. Come on! We haven't all day!"

Down on the other side of the adventure playground Nick suddenly saw what he'd been looking for all the time — the bottle. It was wedged against a stone in the stream. He began to run towards it, forgetting about his class. But he'd also forgotten the bird. It came swooping back from nowhere. It didn't waste a second. It was on him, beak open. It clasped him by his shirt and swept him off his feet.

The bird whirled, making Nick dizzy, and tried to take off. It began to run along the path, trailing Nick between its legs. The bird flapped its wings, grunted deep in its throat, then rose slowly in the air. Nick

stopped struggling. He didn't want to be dropped!

The flight didn't last very long. A giant shadow came speeding along the ground and caught up with them. With a squawk of anger the bird dropped Nick and flapped away. Nick landed on the grass, none too lightly.

"Mark! What are you doing out there, young man?"

"A magpie caught something. I rescued it."

Nick heard Mrs Wright's voice from afar and the voice of his best friend close to.

"What was it?"

"A mouse," Mark called back, loud as a foghorn. "I'll just make sure it's all right, then let it go."

"Don't be too long."

Nick opened his eyes. He was on the very edge of the grass. Mark was kneeling between him and the classroom.

Mark's hand hovered anxiously. "Is that really you, Nick? I saw you from the window."

"That bird's got it in for me," Nick said. "I think it wanted to eat me."

"What?" Mark's whisper boomed. "I can't quite hear. Do you want me to tell Mrs Wright?"

Nick jumped up. "No!" he shouted. "Not yet!"

"Why not?"

Nick had a sudden vision of the awful fuss adults would make about this. "There's a bottle in the stream," he shouted. "Look! You've got to get it and open it for me. Then you'll understand."

"I didn't catch what you said." Mark leant down. "How did you get like this?"

Mrs Wright was at the door again.

"Mark! You can't stay out there. Are you coming?"

"Yes, Mrs Wright." Mark began to straighten up. Then he remembered he had to hide Nick. "When I've done my shoelaces," he called, though he was wearing sandals.

He pretended to fiddle with them. "I can't leave you out here with that magpie about, can I?" he whispered.

Mark was wearing a denim waistcoat. He liked to wear it even in the hottest weather. "Let me climb up," Nick shouted. He hoisted himself onto Mark's knee, then stepped up and grasped his friend's shirt collar. He slid under cover of the waistcoat. Mark turned round and walked towards the school. "But you've still got to get me that bottle!" Nick's muffled voice shouted. "As soon as you can, Mark!"

5

Amos turned the van off the road down through a housing estate. After about half a mile he came to a busy road. He turned left onto it, back in the direction the magpie had taken. Gazza, during their chat, had even mentioned a bottle glinting in the stream at dawn. He was a very observant magpie.

Amos slowed down and scanned the sky for any sign of Gazza. It would be just his luck to lose the genie *and* the bird.

Amos spotted the magpie. The bird was right ahead, about a quarter of a mile away. If their arrangement was working he would be circling over the spot the bottle had floated to. Amos sighed with relief. It was found! Nothing disastrous had happened. He even hummed a little tune to himself. Within ten minutes they should be back on the road home again.

Nick felt deafened. There was a solid wall of sound all around him in the classroom. It wasn't just the voices — and they were bad enough! — it was also all the movements people made: shifting in their chairs, sharpening pencils, knocking things over, the noises Mrs Wright always complained about.

"What's the matter with your arm?" someone asked Mark.

"I've got a stitch," he said.

"I'll tell Mrs Wright," another friend offered.

"No, don't!" Mark said in a panicky way. "It's going off now."

"What happened to the mouse?" another voice asked. "Mrs Wright wouldn't let us come out."

"I let it go. It ran off down the adventure playground."

"Did you see where?"

"Yes."

"Will you show us at dinner time?"

"All right."

Dinner time, Nick thought. Would he have to wait like this till twelve o'clock? He imagined the bottle floating off again, travelling further and further away, and he was sure Mark hadn't grasped how important it was.

It was hot under Mark's arm. Suddenly Nick got an itch. He wriggled. Mark wriggled back. Then Nick became aware of a tremendous noise, like a massive hammer banging next to his ear, like being imprisoned in a bell tower next to the bell. It was his friend's heart beat.

"You are here to work, not talk, Class Six," Mrs Wright said loudly. She gave her desk a little tap. "Get on with your stories, please. I've put plenty of words on the board to help you."

The class quietened, though there was still the odd voice or sound that made Nick wince. In the meantime

Mark had sat down at his table and picked up his pencil. His left elbow firmly holding Nick in place, he got on with writing.

"That's better," Mrs Wright said. "We all ought to have written at least half a dozen lines by now. And I would hope that a lot of you have written more than that."

"Yes."

"Yes, Miss."

"I've written a page."

"I've written two pages."

"No, you haven't."

"That's enough!" Mrs Wright shouted. "I wasn't looking for an answer."

Mark wrote for ten minutes or so. Under his armpit Nick began to stifle. It was so hot he was sure he'd faint any moment. Then Mark whispered, "Hang on!" and got up.

Nick clung on grimly as Mark crossed the room.

"May I go to the toilet, please, Miss?"

Mrs Wright didn't answer straight away. She was hearing a reader.

"Miss! It's desperate!" Mark whined.

That did the trick.

"You'd better hurry," Mrs Wright said. "Off you go."

Nick felt him reach for the door handle, but a girl called out, "Miss, Mark's got something under his arm."

"Who's calling out?" Mrs Wright said. "You know I won't stand for it."

"Emily! Emily!" the children chorused. Emily was a tell-tale.

"Yes, what *is* under your arm, Mark?" Mrs Wright got up. "You're holding yourself oddly."

"Nothing, Miss." Mark turned to hide the bulge Nick was making.

"But you do have something. It's silly to say you haven't when I can see it quite plainly," Mrs Wright said. Nick heard her come across. Mark turned further away from her. "Come on, young man. What's the point of telling fibs? What is it?"

"It's nothing, Miss," Mark said. "Honestly. I was just going to the toilet."

"Mark!" Mrs Wright said. "Why are you telling me a deliberate lie? I've never known you do that before!"

Mark said, "It's — " then stopped.

"It's what?"

"I'm desperate, Miss," Mark said. Nick felt him tremble.

"Unbutton your waistcoat, Mark," Mrs Wright said. "This instant."

Slowly and reluctantly Mark did as he was told. First button. Second button. Third. Fourth. Mark lingered over this one. As he let his hand slip away, Nick wriggled further round under his friend's shoulder.

There was a gasp from the class, then silence. Then someone was shouting and screaming, "A rat! A great big rat wriggling under Mark's waistcoat!"

There followed a din like a thunderstorm.

"What? A rat?" Mrs Wright screeched at Mark. "*Sit down and be quiet, everyone, or I will fetch the*

29

headmaster!" she shouted at the other children. "Tell me, Mark — now — please. I don't mind guinea pigs, but rats — !"

"It isn't one." Mark was close to tears. "I wouldn't have brought an animal in. It's my new Action Doll."

"How could a doll be alive?" Mrs Wright said to the children with relief in her voice. "Let's see it, then, Mark, and get this over with. It's too hot to have all this arguing."

Mark's hand came in after Nick. It grasped him round the waist, rather hard, and tugged. Nick's first impulse was to struggle. Luckily Mark was more in control of himself. He held on to Nick.

"Look, Mrs Wright," he said. "He's ever so lifelike. I meant to show you later as a surprise."

Soft-soaping never did any good with Mrs Wright. "Into my drawer with it," she said. "Then you can go to the toilet." Nick heard her pull the drawer open. In he went.

6

Amos stopped the van and got out. Gazza was swooping and swirling in the sky above a building at the end of the next turning. A school.

"Great!" Amos said. "Mission accomplished." He got back in and drove the van to the end of the school drive. Gazza landed ten metres from him and hopped the rest of the way.

"Qwark!" he said. "Qwark!"

"Hey! You've found it! Well done!" Amos shouted. "Come on in."

"Qwark!"

"Found the bottle but there's something else?"

Gazza explained, darting his head from side to side nervously. He had never been in a vehicle before.

"A boy! Oh, lord! And you say he's gone in the classroom?"

"Qwark!"

Amos had never talked with a magpie before, but he wasn't surprised by its intelligence. Magpies had a bright, quick way about them which he'd always liked.

"I'll tan that child's backside for him when I get hold of him," Amos said. "He's gone too far. Turning himself into a midget! Whatever will they think of next?" He got out of the van and squinted down the stream.

"Qwark!"

"The bottle's just out of sight, you say, where those climbing frames and slides are? A bit tricky that. Every window in the school building looks over it, and it's too big for you to carry."

"Qwark!"

"No, it's not worth trying. And if I dash down there and rescue it, that still leaves the problem of the boy. I can't just leave him. The havoc he might cause doesn't bear thinking about. Let's just hope no grown up sees him. And if they do see him I don't want to get the blame!"

Amos gloomily started the van. "I'll have to think very carefully about what we're going to do now. Oh! if I could just get hold of him! Gazza, I'll tell you what. You keep an eye on the school and that child in particular. I'm going off for a few minutes. I've got a little idea."

The drawer was pitch black. Nick was lying on something. He tried to wriggle off but that made a pile of pencils shift about. This told him which of Mrs Wright's drawers he was in — the middle one with the rulers, pencils, rubbers, drawing pins and compasses. He could feel something extra-sharp at his neck. A compass? He kept very still.

Mrs Wright's voice boomed away above his head. He caught Mark's voice too. ". . . have it back, Miss?" he was saying.

32

"At the end of school, Mark," the teacher replied firmly.

"End of school, Miss?" Mark protested. "But, Miss, you don't realise . . ."

For a moment Nick was afraid Mark would spill the beans.

"Half past three this afternoon," Mrs Wright said. "At the bell. No earlier. Now, don't go on about it."

"Yes, Miss," Mark said faint-heartedly.

"We should be even further into our stories," Mrs Wright announced. "We have had time to write a book by now."

"I've done three pages," a hard worker called out.

"Tony — what about you?"

"Tony's only done three lines, Mrs Wright!" tell-tale Emily called.

"You haven't done any more yourself!" Tony yelled back.

"I was reading — yah!"

"I will not have this calling out!" Mrs Wright bawled. "SILENCE!" Someone added, "In court!" which Mrs Wright either didn't hear or chose to ignore. Silence fell on the class. Mrs Wright called out another reader. The story, a really boring one, began to make Nick yawn. He heard Mrs Wright stifle a yawn too.

When I get hold of that sneaky genie, Nick thought, what I'll say to him! I'll wring his neck! I wonder how he came to be in the stream. Does he belong to someone? And how did he get that odd name, Shybad?

Suddenly a real hubbub broke out in the classroom.

Mrs Wright jumped up. When the tumult had died down Nick heard Mrs Wright say to the class, "I have never seen such a brazen bird in my life. Fancy it peering in like that. I believe I could have touched it through the open window if I'd wanted to. I wonder what interested it so much?"

The dinner bell went half an hour later. The appearance of the magpie at the window had made the class noisy again, and Mrs Wright had been shouting a lot and hammering on the desk top with a ruler. This had deafened Nick. She had said there would be no playtime before dinner because of the horrible row.

Immediately after the bell, however, the class went completely quiet, hoping Mrs Wright would change her mind. She went on hearing a reader for a couple of minutes, then said, "Well, I suppose you'd better go out. That side first." The class tiptoed out of the room then rushed down the corridor. Soon after, Nick could hear everyone screaming and shouting on the adventure playground. He could only hope that Mark had the sense to fetch the bottle straight away. What if someone else reached it first?

Eventually Mrs Wright pushed back her chair and left the classroom. Nick rolled over and very carefully began to kneel up in the darkness. Immediately more pencils began to roll towards him. He found himself thrashing about on top of them. Every movement he made seemed to dislodge more. At last, however, he managed to reach up and touch the top of the drawer.

He pushed on it and pushed, but the drawer was much too heavy for him to shift on his own. He had a moment of panic. He was going to be stuck here till half past three. And if Mark said the wrong thing he would be stuck in here for the night. What should he do — shout for help? Give himself away?

Then someone came into the classroom. Mark? With the bottle? Nick's heart leaped. Yes, it must be him. He could tell from the stealthy way he was moving. The footsteps padded quietly across the room and reached the desk. The drawer above Nick was opened, letting in light, then shut again. Then the drawer Nick was in was wrenched open.

"Ah!" There was a sigh of satisfaction.

Nick blinked his eyes to adjust them to the light. He almost spoke. Then he realised it wasn't Mark standing over him, hand ready to grasp him. Instead of Mark, it was the worst possible person — Basher, the class bully.

Nick sat up in horror. He shouldn't have done that. Basher was pretty stupid but, he wasn't stupid enough to miss a live Action Doll.

"Would you believe it!" Basher exclaimed. "Cor! It's true. They make ones that move on their own! It's live as can be!"

7

Basher wasn't called Basher without reason. He had enormous fists which he'd clobbered Nick with more than once. However the class bully wasn't so brave with 'live' Action Men as with boys three-quarters his size. His hand hovered most uncertainly above Nick.

But Basher wanted Nick badly. Hadn't he taken an enormous risk in sneaking in to play with him? Wouldn't he be the first to be suspected if something went missing? He steeled himself to pick Nick up. His hand came towards the drawer again. When Basher pounced, Nick rolled, hurting himself against the pencils. Basher snatched his hand away as if he'd been bitten. "Ugh!" he said with a shudder.

Nick jumped up and looked over the edge of the drawer. It was a long drop to the floor but he had to do something quickly. Basher was plucking up courage again.

"Come on, you little beauty!" he said, as if talking to a budgie or a guinea pig. "Come on! Come to me!"

Nick decided he'd have to jump. He put a leg over the side of the drawer. Basher pounced again. Nick was grasped round the arms and shoulders. His legs and the lower part of his body were free to wriggle and struggle, but his upper part was in a paralysing grip.

"Got you!" Basher said. "Thought you'd get away from me, did you? You little devil!" He sounded quite affectionate!

Nick had no desire to be stroked or petted by Basher. He did the only thing left to him. He bit one of Basher's fingers as hard as possible.

Basher yelped and dropped him onto Mrs Wright's desk.

"You little devil!" Basher screamed. He sucked at his finger. "I didn't mean any harm. I'll get you for that! You better not be poisonous!" Nick ducked as an unfriendly hand just missed him. The draught nearly bowled him over. He didn't wait any longer. He leaped down onto Mrs Wright's chair — there was a cushion on the seat which softened his fall — quickly sat on the chair edge and lowered himself towards the floor. Basher's foot came sliding past, trying to knock him over. Nick darted under Mrs Wright's desk.

Outside, the bell rang for the second sitting of dinner. In a couple of minutes thirty children would come pouring into the room to fetch their money and sandwich boxes. Nick ran for it, straight up the first row of desks, right to the back of the classroom. There he dodged behind one of the tables — in fact the one he usually sat at. Then he ducked down and began to work his way towards the front of the classroom again.

Basher came thumping after Nick, even though he'd lost sight of him. He stood half-way up the room, close enough for Nick to hear him swearing under his breath. His ankles were just below Nick's nose. His dusty black shoes could have crushed him with one

38

kick. Then to Nick's horror Basher got down on his knees.

All of a sudden Mrs Wright came into the room. "Who said you could come in here on your own, Brian?" she asked Basher. "You know you aren't allowed."

"Er," Basher said. "Please, Miss — "

"Well," Mrs Wright said impatiently. "Well?"

"I was chasing . . ." Basher stopped. How could he say it? *I was chasing a live Action Doll!* No one could say that and expect anyone, especially Mrs Wright, to believe him.

"Why are you kneeling, Brian? Stand up at once!" Mrs Wright snapped.

"Brian! I'm warning you!" Mrs Wright said. Her feet advanced up the row towards Basher. "Stand up and tell me what you're doing in here!"

Nick saw Basher jerk up as Mrs Wright's high heels came near. He took his chance to move away across two more rows of desks. Now he was at the side of the room and near the door to the corridor. He squeezed himself into the space between a cupboard and the wall. He wished now he'd asked that stupid genie to make him even smaller!

With a great clatter the class began to come into the room. A fraction of a second later Mrs Wright discovered her middle drawer was open.

"Are you responsible for this?" she asked Basher. The children continued to pour in.

"What's he done, Miss?" they all asked.

"Taken Mark's Action Doll by the look of it," Mrs

Wright said.

There was an agonised wail from Mark. "What's he done with him, Miss? Where's he gone?"

"It ran away from me, Miss," Basher said. Someone tittered, then everyone began to laugh. "But it did!" Basher shouted tearfully. "When I picked it up it bit me. Then it jumped down on the floor and ran towards the back of the room. Honest, Miss!" The laughter died down a little.

"Bit you?" Lisa said. "Where?"

Basher held out his hand. Mrs Wright said, "That does look like a bite. Is there an animal in here?"

"Ask Mark," Basher said in a sulky voice. "It's his, not mine."

"The whole point is that it's Mark's, not yours, Brian," Mrs Wright said, "wherever you got that cut from. Though funnily enough it does look like a set of miniature tooth marks." She shut the drawer of her desk. "Hurry up, children, please. And, Brian, could we have the Action Man back? You've been caught doing something very silly."

"I can't, Miss. It ran off," Basher insisted.

"But, Brian!"

One of the girls screamed.

"Mrs Wright! Look! There! Behind the cupboard! Something's moving!"

8

The girl's scream made all the other girls scream and the boys shout. Mrs Wright managed to get her voice above the rest but not to quieten them. "Be careful, Miss! You don't want to get bitten like Basher did!" Emily screeched.

Nick crawled right under the cupboard: and only just in time. The next thing he heard was Mrs Wright's voice booming down the back of the cupboard: "What are you talking about? I can't see anything."

It was disgusting underneath the cupboard, all dust and ends of crayons and last year's crisp packets.

Nick heard Mrs Wright move away. Perhaps he would be all right. Then suddenly he had the sensation of being watched. He swung round. Someone was kneeling down with their head to the floor.

"It moved, Miss! I swear it did! It's under there! Do something, Miss!" the voice demanded. "Ugh! It's horrid!"

Nick recognised the face which immediately disappeared. It was Emily's. Trust her!

Other faces appeared, among them Mrs Wright's.

"It's Mark's Action Doll all right," Mrs Wright said. "Brian — tell me the truth. What bit you?"

"That did, Miss!" Basher said sulkily.

"It's not moving though, is it?" Mrs Wright's upside-down voice said. "Oh, this is so silly, kneeling on the floor discussing whether a toy's alive! I'm going to fetch the caretaker to move the cupboard and get it out. Now, let's have an end to this. Off to your dinner, everyone. You'll be holding up the whole school."

She gave Nick one last look as someone shoved a metre stick under the cupboard and tried to sweep him out. Nick drew back to avoid a nasty blow.

"It moved! I saw it! I saw it myself!" Mrs Wright's face withdrew. "I'm going to get the headmaster!" she called. "Out of my way! Don't panic, anyone! Just stay where you are! Freeze!"

In a phone box near the school Amos was saying to his wife, "I just thought I'd let you know how I was getting on." He told her about Nick. "The little devil's in the school somewhere. Wait till I get my hands on him. Gazza's keeping a lookout. Gazza? That's the magpie. You'll like him. He's coming back with me. He's got no ties around here. Now I must ring off. I'm running out of coins and I've another phone call to make when I've found the number."

In Mrs Wright's classroom all hell was let loose. A succession of faces pushed down to the bottom of the cupboard. Other faces pushed them aside.

Nick took a big decision. He wriggled out from underneath and stood behind the cupboard which

42

swayed backwards and forwards with everyone leaning on it. The faces looked down at him from above now, some of them excited, some of them rather frightened.

"What is it really, Mark?"

"Mark, tell us."

"Did you know, Mark?"

"It looks almost human!"

"I told you it bit me!" Basher protested in a hurt way. "No one would believe me!"

Nick thought, There's nothing for it. I shall have to put them out of their misery, and before Mrs Wright comes back too. He edged along the back of the cupboard and stepped out into the open.

There was an ooh! and an ah! and everyone stepped back. A solid semi-circle formed around him. He looked up. The class looked at him. He could have been an alien from another planet!

"Well," he said, "it's me."

Thirty heads were lowered towards him.

He shouted at the top of his voice, "It's me — Nick. I found a genie. He shrank me."

The faces looked at him, mystified.

"It can talk," a voice said from the back. "What did it say?"

Nick felt rather irritated, for he'd expected them to be impressed. He took another step towards them. All of them took a step back.

"I'm Nick from your class — you remember me, surely?"

Still no one seemed to understand. For a moment he wondered whether they'd forgotten who he was —

perhaps the genie had managed to wipe him from their memories. But Mark had recognised him, hadn't he? He took another step forward. The children retreated again, shoving back the desks to keep at a safe distance.

Suddenly Mark pushed his way to the front. "Look," he said. "It's Nick from our class — who sits next to me. My best friend. You know him. Don't be stupid."

"How can it be?" a girl said. "He's all small."

"He can't help being small," Mark said. "He's in trouble. No one would choose to be like this, would they?"

"I wouldn't mind," Basher said. "It would be fun. I could go around — " he looked at Nick, " — biting people. There was no need to bite me," he said.

"But how did he get like that?" another girl said.

"I expect it was the magpie," Mark said, "the one that was trying to get in the window. It wasn't a mouse I was trying to rescue from it, but Nick." He pointed.

"But it was a genie! Its bottle's down in the stream!" Nick shouted. "Listen, will you?"

"He's talking again," one of the boys said. "What's he saying?"

"A magpie? I don't believe that." Adrian, the hardest-working person in the class, suddenly pushed to the front. "A mad scientist or someone like that's done it to him." He knelt down in front of Nick. "Now, shut up, everyone! Let's hear what he's trying to say. It was a mad scientist, wasn't it?"

But it was too late. Mrs Wright was coming back up the corridor, her voice loud in explanation to someone.

45

"Quick!" Mark said. "I'll carry you out." He scooped Nick up and went to the door.

"She'll see him!" someone said.

"The headmaster's with her," another added.

Mark reached into his pocket. "It's clean," he said, as if it mattered. He threw his handkerchief round Nick.

"Where are you going, Mark?" It was Mrs Wright. "What have you got in your hand? *That?* Give it here!"

Nick found himself being dumped on the floor. He disentangled himself from the handkerchief.

"Quick! Run!" Mark hissed. "I'll keep an eye out for you." He gave Nick a shove that sent him flying.

"What are you doing, Mark?" the headmaster said. "What is it? It's very tiny. A baby monkey? Oh dear, I've got the wrong glasses on."

"It's what I told you about, Headmaster!" Mrs Wright screeched. "If only you'd listened to me and come sooner, it wouldn't have escaped."

Nick ran past the cloakroom and toilets. He then turned right into what they called the short corridor. It was a mistake. Left would have taken him to the front doors of the school, which were open.

He pulled up to run back, but the door at the end of the short corridor began to open, and he had to dart in through an open doorway next to him. He gazed around wildly, spotted some floor-length curtains and hid behind them.

Above his head the telephone rang. It sounded as loud as a burglar alarm. He was in the headmaster's study.

Mrs Bate came into the room. "Crossley Primary School," she said. "Good morning. Can I help you? The headmaster? Yes, he is in. Who's speaking, please? A moment. I'll try to find him."

Nick heard his class going into dinner. They were discussing what had happened at the tops of their voices. He heard his own name mentioned.

The headmaster was coming, Mrs Wright with him. "I assure you, Headmaster," Mrs Wright was saying tearfully, "I saw this doll with my own eyes. I saw Mark putting it in my drawer. Then it was moving under my cupboard. It was the same doll we both saw running down the corridor."

"I am not denying anything or calling you a liar, Mrs Wright. It's just that I am very confused and also very short-sighted. Yes, who is it?" the headmaster said into the phone. "I suggest we talk in a minute, Mrs Wright, about what has happened. Who did you say?" he asked the person on the phone in a puzzled way. "I don't quite follow what you want. A Mr Hamish? This afternoon you say? Booked to appear here? But it's not in my diary. I didn't book you. Oh, it's a free show, you say? Not a sausage to pay? That's different of course. Well, I don't see why not. We could all do with a spot of entertainment. Thank you. Half past one, you say? Yes, Mr Hamish. I look forward to seeing you."

The headmaster put the phone down. "How nice," he said. "An afternoon off. How pleasant!" Then his voice became more serious. "Now, Mrs Wright. Let's go for a little walk together to your classroom while your children are in dinner and sort all this out."

Nick crept to the door. He had to escape from the school as soon as possible. No one here was going to help him find the genie.

He didn't notice the magpie gazing in through the study window.

9

From the door of the headmaster's study Nick looked up and down the corridor. What was the best thing to do? Try and escape through the school front door? Or the staffroom window? It had been open. The danger was Mrs Bate, who did her typing in there, and of course the teachers themselves. But Nick knew most of them didn't go into the staffroom till later.

He decided to take the chance. He ran down the corridor, into the staffroom, and took cover under the first chair he came to. Mrs Bate's feet were sticking out from under her desk. He could hear her typing.

The window was still open. A quick dash when she wasn't looking, a scramble up onto the easy chair directly opposite him, and he was practically out.

Just as he was set to go, the headmaster came pounding down the corridor and through the door. He drew forward the chair that Nick was hiding underneath and sat down. Nick had to jump forward to stay under it.

"What on earth do you make of this business in Mrs Wright's classroom?" he asked Mrs Bate. "Mrs Wright is the last teacher I'd have suspected of seeing fairies."

"Very true, Headmaster," Mrs Bate said. "Not many fairies at the bottom of *her* garden."

"Unfortunately I didn't have my right glasses on or apparently I would have seen this remarkable creature. Mrs Wright says it ran right past me. I must admit I did see something moving, but it could have been a garden gnome roller-skating for all I know." He sighed deeply. "My wife's always saying I need new glasses."

"Yes, Headmaster," Mrs Bate said with a sigh of her own. She wanted to finish this letter so she could go for her own dinner. She typed a few more words.

"I can hardly call Mrs Wright a liar," the headmaster went on, "but I shall be the laughing-stock of the whole town if I call the police."

"The police!"

"That's what Mrs Wright is saying I should do."

"Goodness me!" Mrs Bate said. "That docs seem to be going a little far."

"But what," the headmaster said, "if Mrs Wright and her class really did see it? They certainly saw something. They're saying it's Nick, one of Mrs Wright's children, who went to the dentist. I checked in the register. He certainly hasn't come back."

"It's an awful problem," Mrs Bate sympathised. "I don't know what to think. By the way, where is it supposed to be now?" More interest came into her voice. "This thing. Where?"

"Down this way, I think," the headmaster said.

Mrs Bate drew up her feet.

"I hate mice!" she whispered.

"Good lord, Mrs Bate! This isn't some mouse we're talking about," the headmaster said. "It's much larger!"

That seemed to make it worse. Mrs Bate's feet hit the ground again. Her chair went flying backwards and over. Her feet rushed past Nick's face and her heels clattered up the corridor as she part-screamed, part-shouted, "And you leave me down here all on my own, when you know there's something on the loose!"

"Goodness me! Goodness me!" the headmaster exclaimed. He got up and quickly followed her out. "Mrs Bate! Come back!" he called.

Nick ran across the floor towards the chair he had to climb. It was the kind of chair called an easy chair, but it wasn't easy to climb. The seat was way above his head and it was covered in a slippery material. He was still trying to get a grip when there were voices in the corridor again. Quickly he crawled under the chair — there wasn't quite enough space for him to stand up.

The headmaster came back into the room with Miss Bester, the deputy headmistress.

"Personally I think Mrs Wright is going potty!" Miss Bester was saying. "Whoever heard such rubbish!"

"Oh dear, I just don't know," the headmaster answered. He sat heavily on the chair Nick was hidden under. It sagged and bumped Nick's head. Miss Bester went to fill the kettle. The headmaster laughed. "It would be nice in a way if it were true!"

"If what were true?" Miss Bester said.

"That you could shrink children," the headmaster said. "Think how handy it would be. No more coaches to go to the swimming baths — just drive down in your own car with all your class on the back seat. Or I could hold assembly on top of my desk."

Miss Bester wasn't much struck with the idea.

"They're trouble enough as they are," she complained.

After that there was a long silence, in which the only sounds were those made by Miss Bester as she brewed the tea and by the headmaster yawning rather loudly.

The headmaster yawned again. Nick saw Miss Bester's feet and heard the clink of china. As the headmaster took his cup of tea a pen fell from his pocket onto the floor. It rolled under the chair, stopping at Nick's feet. The headmaster's hand followed the pen. His fingers groped for it. They missed the pen, but the tips touched Nick on the face. "It must have rolled right to the back," he complained. "Oh bother! I'll have to pull the chair out. There's something else down there too." He stood up. Nick crawled backwards so that he was wedged right up against the skirting board. He didn't see how he could avoid discovery.

"Have you phoned Nick's parents yet," Miss Bester asked, "to see what's really become of him?"

"Nick? Oh yes. I tried a moment ago. Perhaps I ought to try again."

"Why don't you?" Miss Bester said. "It would put an end to this silly business."

"Yes," the headmaster said. "Remind me to get my pen." He walked towards the door, then stopped. "That's an interesting bottle on Mrs Bate's desk. I wonder where it came from. I'll have a closer look when I come back."

10

Nick crawled forward again. He was trembling with excitement. How had he missed it? Yes, there it was, next to Mrs Bate's typewriter — the genie bottle! Someone had brought it in!

I've got to get hold of Mark, he thought, someone I can trust to open it for me. I'm not trying to open it again myself. But how will I get hold of Mark? I'm trapped in here.

Suddenly half a dozen more teachers invaded the staffroom. Nick shrank back out of sight. One of them was Mrs Wright. She still looked upset.

"It's all very well for you to laugh," she was saying, "but I'm the one who saw it."

The headmaster followed them in.

"Still not in," he said.

"Who's not in?" one of the teachers asked.

"Nick's parents. I've been trying to phone them."

"Oh, the lad who's supposed to have turned into a midget!"

There was a general laugh.

"Just the kind of thing he would get up to!" said Mr Price, who took games.

"I really would like to know what's happened to young Nick," the headmaster said.

Suddenly the teachers were talking about the bottle.

"It was handed in to the dinner ladies," one of them said.

"Anything in it?" another asked.

"They couldn't get the cork out."

"Have you tried?"

"No, I haven't. Wait a minute. I'll have a go. No, I can't move it either."

"Give it here."

That was Mr Price.

"Nearly got it," he said. "But not quite. Someone's super-glued it."

"It's really stuck," another said.

Oh no! Nick thought. Please, please don't get it open! Life would just get too complicated.

The headmaster had the bottle now. He tugged at the cork, going redder and redder in the face.

"Almost, but not quite," he said. "Here, Miss Bester. You try. You've strong wrists."

He passed it to her.

Miss Bester managed it. The cork came out.

"Ugh! What a nasty smell!" she said, her nose a couple of centimetres from the top. She pushed the cork straight back in. "Someone throw it away!"

The headmaster took it from her and put it in the wastepaper basket just as there was a knock at the door. "Funny, the things children find," he said.

Only Nick seemed to have seen the faint wisp of smoke that had risen from the neck of the bottle.

"Yes! Who is it?" the headmaster called.

A boy from the top class opened the door. "The cook

says the staff dinners are ready," he announced.

"And about time too," Mr Price said. "I'm famished." He led the way from the room.

The last teacher had hardly gone before Nick was across the carpet and by the wastepaper basket. It took all his strength but he managed to hoist himself onto the rim. He grasped the cork and pulled. It came out easily — he'd seen that Miss Bester had not put it back in very carefully.

Nothing happened for a second, then in a great rush the genie shot out and billowed above Nick's head.

"Was that you," it shouted, "disturbing me again? Do you realise you nearly cut off my head when you put the cork back in?" Everything was livid about it — its colour, its voice, the expression on its face.

"Of course it wasn't me! How could it have been with me this size? And I want my other two wishes!" Nick shouted. He felt almost as angry as the genie.

Shybad said something very rude.

"You've got to give them to me. You said so yourself."

"Smell, do I? Think I didn't hear, did you? I'm not deaf, you know. I'll pay you back."

"It wasn't me," Nick said. "And you know it. What other people say's not my fault. I want my second wish. And I don't want any tricks this time."

"Bet you want to be turned back to normal size," the genie sneered. "Shybad could have told you it was a mistake the moment you made your first wish."

This wish had been on the very tip of Nick's tongue. He choked it back.

"Well, come on! Come on! I'm not waiting any longer!" the genie said. "There's a limit to my patience and I've reached it."

"You're trying to rush me," Nick said, "to make me say something stupid. I know what you're up to. Are all genies as bad-tempered as you?"

"Good lord!" Mr Price said from the doorway.

Nick froze. The genie did much the same.

"What's the matter? Come on — you're blocking the doorway," Miss Bester said from behind him in the corridor.

Mr Price wasn't able to move. He stood holding his dinner-tray, with his eyes glued to Nick.

"It's Nick," he said. "I'd recognise him anywhere. And a funny sort of red cloud."

With a snarl the genie shrank back into its bottle pulling the cork after it as before. Mr Price's eyes followed this with amazement.

"Come on!" Miss Bester said. "This dinner wasn't very hot to begin with."

"What's the hold up?" another teacher's voice complained.

The genie popped the cork back out.

"Unless you want to give up, you better wish you could fly," it said without appearing again.

Mr Price's eyes nearly popped out of his head.

"I do," Nick said without thinking.

"Never in a thousand years have I met such a troublesome wish-maker," the genie said. Unexpectedly it laughed, then with a grim chuckle it corked itself again.

Fly? Nick thought. How?

He waved his arms experimentally.

"Nick's flying now!" Mr Price announced in a shout. "Hey! Come back!"

11

As Nick flew out through the gap in the net curtains, his foot tangled in the hair of a dinner-lady standing just outside the window. She swatted at him. Winded, he flew up till he was at the level of the flat school roof.

"You could have killed me!" he shouted as she glared around.

Mr Price stuck his head out of the staffroom window.

"Did anyone see a flying child?" he shouted in great excitement. "Listen, everyone — "

"A great big dragonfly got tangled in my hair, if that's what you mean," the dinner-lady said. "It gave me the shock of my life!"

"Where did it go?"

"Where? I don't know!"

"Oh, Mr Price! You're making a fool of yourself!" came Miss Bester's voice.

Nick flew out of sight over the school roof. He wasn't sure how he did it. It felt a bit like swimming without having to use your legs. But thinking about it was a mistake — he began to lose the knack. Down and down he sank until his feet were skimming the surface of the roof. Suddenly he crash-landed in the sticky tarmac.

That genie! he thought angrily as he sat up. It's managed to trick me again. I never wanted to fly. I wasted that wish. Now I'll have to use the last one to get back to my proper size, and I won't have got anything out of my three wishes, none of the usual things like wealth, health and happiness.

Nick's dejection didn't last long. Flying was fun.

He stood up in the tar — it had softened in the hot sun and was like warmish treacle — raised his arms, tugged his feet free and flew again.

He flew about a metre above roof top level towards the opposite side of the school and landed on the cooling-tower above the boiler room. Wow! He could see for miles. He could see his own house on the edge of the estate, and behind it the fields where he played after school. He could even see the winding course of the stream.

His eye travelled from the fields, over the main road and down to the school drive. At this moment half a dozen children were coming back from dinners at home. They were passing a black van parked near the drive. Nick stared at it. What was written on its side? He shaded his eyes. AMOS something. AMOS EN-TER — AMOS ENTERTAINMENTS.

Where now? He fancied flying across to some trees on the far side of the playground. They looked shady. To avoid being spotted from the school, however, he would have to fly very high and he wasn't sure he liked the idea of that. Courage. Why not? He stood, raised his arms and launched himself. A pair of sparrows came flitting past. Nick shouted at them and they

nearly dropped from the air with amazement. Then a great shadow passed over him.

Nick glanced up and his heart nearly stopped. He flew to one side but the shadow changed direction and followed him. He dodged about — right, left, backwards, forwards. No good. The magpie was practically on top of him.

In his panic Nick grounded himself in the tar on the roof top again. As he knelt up with a squelch the magpie landed a couple of metres away. It began to strut towards him, carefully picking its claws from the tar with each step. Nick raised his arms but it was no use — the power to fly seemed to have deserted him again.

Closer and closer the magpie came. "Qwark!" it shouted. "Qwark! Qwark!"

What a way to go, he thought, a magpie's dinner! No Mark to rescue me this time.

The magpie stopped, head on one side. We've been through this before, Nick thought. Get it over with. There didn't seem to be anything he could do.

Then suddenly, for some reason, the magpie's gaze had shifted behind him.

"Qwark!" it shouted at Nick, almost like a warning.

Nick stared at the bird. What on earth did it want now? One moment it wanted to eat him, the next —

He jerked himself round. A cat was delicately padding its way across the roof, the sleek, fat, well-fed cat that belonged to the caretaker. Dinner, it was thinking.

Nick didn't wait to find out whether the cat would

realise he was human before it was too late. He began running. To his surprise the magpie didn't try to stop him but hopped right over him towards the cat, squawking as if encouraging Nick to get away. The cat leaped, landing where Nick had been a second before. The magpie fell on it.

Nick half ran across the roof and found he was half flying too. A tremendous argument began in the background — hisses and growls from the cat, squawks and harsh menacing clicks from the magpie.

He came to the edge of the roof sooner than he'd expected. He tumbled over it. The ground came up to meet him. Less than a metre from it, perhaps only half a metre, his arms found the right rhythm. He was really flying again.

But where was he? He was surrounded by four walls, two of them mainly window. There was an open door he seemed to recognise.

Then he realised where he was — in the enclosed play area for the reception class between Miss Bester's room and the hall.

Both cat and magpie peered over the edge of the roof. Nick flew through the open door, across Miss Bester's room, out into a corridor, down it, and into the hall which was full of children finishing their dinner. With an immense effort he flew up towards the ceiling. He found a place to rest on the top of the curtains and drew breath. What a close shave that had been. At least there was nothing in here that would eat him!

12

Below Nick half a dozen cooks and dinner-ladies were chatting and collecting chairs and tables and sweeping the floor, when the bell for afternoon school rang. At the same time the headmaster came into the hall and said, "I don't like to hurry you, ladies, but a gentleman is bringing his theatre company here this afternoon. I promised him the hall for half past one."

It took a few minutes for the dinner ladies to finish. Then they pulled back the shutters that separated the hall from the kitchen and everything went very quiet.

Nick looked across at the hall clock. Just gone twenty past one. Everyone would be in their class-rooms now. Wouldn't now probably be the best time to sneak into the staffroom to get his third and final wish — to be made his proper size again? Was it any use pretending the genie was ever going to give him a wish that would do him any good? When he'd got back to proper size, and all the explanations had been made, he could come in with the other children and watch the play.

He was just preparing to glide down from his hiding-place, rather nervously because he still hadn't really mastered this flying business, when he heard a vehicle pull up with a squeal of brakes outside the school. A few seconds later the school front door opened.

Nick hesitated and it was lucky he did so, for the visitor came straight into the hall. He walked into the middle and stood there. Then he slowly turned round to inspect every corner. Nick closed his eyes as the stranger's gaze even travelled up to where he was hiding.

"So nice to meet you!" The headmaster came rushing into the hall. He thrust a hand out. "Good afternoon, Mr Hamish!"

The man took the headmaster's hand.

"Mr *Amos*, actually," he said. "But people usually call me plain Amos."

Suddenly Nick began to take a great deal of interest. That sinister black van out on the road must have been his. What did he want here?

"Amos — oh, I'm so sorry," the headmaster said.

"I was just looking around," Amos said, "to see where we had to perform. I've one or two things to bring in. Then I'll be all ready to start." He pointed to a corner. "Most of my stuff will be there. And I'll put a chalk mark round two areas where the children must not go under any circumstances. You can bring them down in ten minutes."

The headmaster seemed puzzled. "Are you on your own then, Mr Amos?" he asked. "Theatre companies usually have more than one person."

"Just me. Oh, and my magic as well, of course!" Amos laughed. "That makes a big difference."

"Ah, magic!" The headmaster laughed too. "Is there

anything I can do to help? Would you like me to round up some strong lads to help with the fetching and carrying?"

"Very kind," Amos said, "but I'll manage."

"No trouble at all, I assure you," the headmaster said. "The boys would be only too eager. They'd consider it an honour."

"All the same," Amos said, "I would prefer to move things myself. I know children like to help, but I have some rather delicate equipment."

"Oh!" the headmaster said. "Then I'll send a message round to the classes that they should come down in about ten minutes."

"Good," Amos said, still staring all round the hall. Nick leant forward to see him better. He didn't look sinister — rather pleasant and a bit scruffy, dressed in jeans and a tee-shirt.

As soon as the headmaster had gone, Amos dug into the pockets of his jeans. He took out a piece of chalk, walked nearly to the other end of the hall, bent down, and drew a circle on the floor. Then he straightened up, came back and drew another, larger circle in one of the corners. Then he ran the chalk between the two circles and back again. He'd made a sort of path across the hall. He stood back, looked at what he'd done, said to himself, "It'll have to do," and went out.

He returned with a largish wicker basket which he placed in the circle next to the curtains where Nick was still hiding. Something stirred in the basket. "Sshh!" Amos hissed. "I'm sorry about this but you'll be out soon enough." He went out of the hall again.

66

When he returned he had two ordinary carrier bags in each hand. They didn't look particularly full but Amos carried them as if they were very heavy. He put two down outside the chalk marks and the other two by the basket in the circle. He knelt and took a bottle from one of them.

Nick craned forward, then went cold. The bottle was *his*, the one that had been in the staffroom the last time he'd seen it. He wanted to cry out to stop him, but Amos was too fast — he uncorked the bottle.

Nothing happened.

"Oh! Come on! I know you're in there. Wake up, do!" Amos snapped. "This is an emergency."

Nick scarcely breathed. What was he trying to do? Put the genie in a worse temper still?

Amos put the bottle on the floor. "All I need's a hand setting this stuff up, nothing that'll tire you — and a bit of acting afterwards."

A shape hung above the bottle, but it wasn't Shybad's shape, and it was purple, not red.

"I was dreaming," a voice complained from mid-air. "I was dreaming of a holiday."

"Huh!" Amos said. "I'm finding it a bit hectic too, with your friend Shybad on the loose and you pretending to be asleep. I tried to wake you once before, remember?"

Shybad's his genie! Nick thought.

"No friend of mine!" the voice said. "And I don't know what you mean about pretending."

"Oh! Come on!" Amos said. "Behaving like that's given me enough trouble already. We've got to put on

67

a good show. We aren't even booked in for this school. We're not making a penny out of it."

"What are we doing here, then?" the voice asked. It was deep and musical, rather pleasant to hear, and quite different from Shybad's cross tones. "Don't blame me if you like extra work. Perhaps you'll be able to afford garage mechanics in the future for your priceless van."

"One of the little blighters who goes to this school has got hold of Shybad," Amos said. "Gazza found the child running around reduced to fifteen centimetres high. Oh, you don't know Gazza, do you? He's a magpie, and a very sensible magpie at that."

Magpie! Nick thought. *That magpie! It had something to do with this man?*

"Nushing, the only one of you three genies who might be described as sensible, introduced me to Gazza. He and I have been chasing this child all morning. Some people go wild with three wishes. Heaven help him when I get my hands on that child!"

Me? Nick thought. *I didn't mean to cause any trouble. I didn't know it was his genie. It never said.*

"I pity him," the voice said from mid-air. "Your anger is terrible, O Amos! Where is the child now? Quivering in some snake-ridden pit? I only ask out of polite interest."

"In the school somewhere. Why else are we here? Gazza had to rescue him from a cat half an hour ago. *And* he seems to have learnt to fly. He's a tricky little devil. But it's Shybad I'm worried about. His bottle was in the stream till not so long ago, but now it's

68

disappeared. Likely as not this lad's hidden it somewhere. Right — " He glanced at his watch. "We've
only a few minutes left."

Amos went over to one of the carrier bags and took
out a screen larger than the bag itself. He and a shape
Nick could see only dimly, carried it between them to
the far circle. "Right. Now the sides." They returned
to the bag and produced two more pieces of scenery,
both of them taller than the tall figure of Amos himself.
"Thanks," he said, when he and the shape had
assembled what turned out to be a fantastically
decorated castle with turrets at each corner.

"And how did Shybad come to disappear?" the deep
voice asked. It was just below Nick.

"As if you didn't know!" Amos exclaimed. "After
your midnight argument in the lay-by he must have
been in such a foul temper that he twitched his bottle
over and it rolled out of the back of the van. Somehow
it got in the stream. Gazza saw it early in the morning.
It floated down this way. It was lucky I hadn't gone
any further when I missed him."

"Depends how you look upon it," the genie said
thoughtfully.

"Next time both of you stay at home!" Amos
snapped. "There are other genies where you come
from."

More! Nick thought.

Amos brought the other two shopping-bags into the
nearer chalk circle and pulled more screens out of
them. Invisible hands helped him build. He rum-
maged in one of the bags. "Drat! I seem to have

forgotten the flag to go on top," he said.

"It is behind you," the genie said.

"Ah yes," Amos said as he picked up a splendid banner from the bare floor. He passed it up. "Thank you." The invisible hands adjusted it. The banner flowed as if there were real winds blowing. There appeared a magnificent palace which seemed to be larger than the hall in which it stood.

"They come," the invisible creature said. He chuckled. "Lots of little devils!"

"We're just in time, then," Amos said. "Thank you for your help. Perhaps when it's all over — "

"I'm hardly likely to go to sleep in the next hour," the voice said with a sigh. The cork popped back into the bottle.

Nick had no time to tell Amos he'd got it all wrong about him and the genie. The first class invaded the hall.

13

The headmaster rushed in and overtook the first children.

"All right, Mr Amos?" he inquired. "Children! Stand still where you are, please."

"Yes, ready, thank you," Amos said, giving a little bow in the headmaster's direction.

"And where are we supposed to sit?" the headmaster inquired. He gave the scenery a startled look.

"Oh, anywhere outside the chalk lines," Amos replied. "Just as long as the children don't cross them. We don't want anything happening to them, do we?" He turned away from the headmaster with a wink and disappeared inside the palace.

More children began to flood in from the other end of the hall. "No one inside the chalk lines," the headmaster cried. "Otherwise, teachers, you may sit your children where you like." He gave the palace another amazed stare.

"Over here, my class," Miss Bester said. "*And that includes you, Jeremy Thompson!*"

The space around the chalk lines began to fill up. Nick's own class filed in with an upset-looking Mrs Wright at the front, hand in hand with a furious-looking Basher.

71

"Anywhere, anywhere, Mrs Wright!" the headmaster said. Mr Price's class arrived too. Mr Price looked very thoughtful.

Now the hall was full. A hush fell.

Suddenly the palace and castle lit up. The children gasped at its splendour. Just as their gasps died away Amos stepped out of the palace. He was no longer in his jeans, sandals and tee-shirt. He wore a magnificent golden and purple robe. There was a crown on his head, studded with shining jewels. His face was different too. He had a strong black beard.

The children began to gasp again, but Amos stilled them with a wave of his hand.

"Children and teachers," he said, "you are going to see a play, the like of which you have never seen before and perhaps will never see again. How will the marvellous things you'll see be made? I'll let you into a secret. By magic!" The children laughed and the teachers smiled knowingly. Amos laughed too. "You don't believe me, do you?" he shouted. "You don't believe in magic, do you?" The children shouted no, but a few shouted yes, mostly the younger ones.

"Well, make up your minds!" Amos laughed. "Do you believe in magic or not?"

This time more children shouted yes.

Amos laughed, a wickedly infectious laugh. "Well, you'll believe in magic before I've done with you! I guarantee that!"

He swung round, pointed a finger at the wicker basket and called, "Gazza!" The lid of the basket flew open and out strutted not a magpie but a magnificent golden-feathered eagle. The bird hopped off the ground with an easy flap of its wings and landed on Amos' shoulders.

"Who believes in magic now?" Amos asked with a tremble of a laugh in his voice.

"We do!" the children all shouted. "We do!"

"All of you?" Amos demanded.

"Yes!" the children shouted. "All of us."

Nick shouted with them.

Miss Bester leant across and said something to the headmaster. She had a very concerned look on her face. The headmaster looked across towards Amos. He was going to get up, but Amos said:

"If we want to see some real magic I think it might be better if all the grown ups went to sleep during the performance." He snapped his fingers. The teachers' heads drooped and before Nick's eyes they fell asleep.

There was a great cheer from the children, then complete silence.

Amos pointed towards the castle he had built at the far end. The lights of the castle grew brighter still.

A door in its side flew open. There was a fanfare of trumpets. Amos beckoned and out of the castle stepped a beautiful princess. If the children were amazed to find she'd been hiding in there, Nick was even more amazed. He had seen the castle grow from nothing. He knew no girl had gone in.

"Meet the Princess Ching Feng," Amos intoned, "imprisoned in the lonely castle of Pekin by the wicked magician, Fo Long." Impossible as it might seem, another figure stepped from the castle, a black-robed

73

figure. It seized Ching Feng by the arm and pulled her back inside. The door shut behind them and the lights of the castle dimmed. All looked towards Amos again.

"Children," he said in a low, soothing voice which calmed those who had been upset by the sight of the wicked magician. "Children, I — Ching Feng's father, together with my faithful eagle, Gazza, mean to rescue Ching Feng. That is the story we are going to tell you today. But first I must introduce my servant, Nushing." Out of his pocket Amos pulled a lamp.

"A lamp!" he cried. He laughed. "A lamp!" The children sighed. "Whatever use is a lamp to me? I shall throw it away. It doesn't even seem a very good one."

"No! No!" the children cried.

"No?" Amos cried in return. "No? Why not?"

"Use it!" a voice called.

"How?" Amos demanded. "I have no oil. How shall I light it?"

"Rub it!" the children cried.

"Rub it!" Amos said in blank amazement. "Why, it's a filthy thing. I'll get my hands dirty."

"Don't be so stupid! Rub it and see!" Mr Price suddenly called. He rose drowsily to his feet. The headmaster stirred. Miss Bester twitched.

"Back to sleep!" Amos commanded Mr Price. Mr Price slumped back in his chair, asleep.

"Shall I rub it?" he asked the children.

"Yes!" they all shouted.

"Then rub it I shall!" Amos said. He pulled from his robes a splendidly embroidered handkerchief. He rubbed the lamp. There was a hush and then, from

75

outside the school it seemed, there came a crack of
thunder. Out of the spout of the lamp there grew
another genie, the third genie Nick had seen that day.
It grew from nothing until it almost filled the hall. It
was a beautiful genie, made of every colour under the
sun.

It bowed towards Amos.

"What is your command, O Master?" it asked.

Bewitched, Nick gazed out. This must be Nushing,
he thought, the other genie Amos had mentioned.

"Let the play commence!" Amos commanded.

Nick found his eyes were closing. "But I must stay
awake," he thought. "I can't miss this. It's too good.
And if that genie who gave me my wishes belongs to
him, and if I fall asleep and he's gone by the time I
wake up — "

His eyes closed.

14

Nick woke up. He felt cold. He rubbed his eyes and sat up. For a moment he couldn't think where he was. Then he remembered Amos and the play, the magnificent palace and the castle, Ching Feng and the wicked magician Fo Long, the eagle Gazza, and Nushing, the multi-coloured genie of the lamp. He was still on the curtain, and he looked down and saw that it hadn't all been a dream and that he really was tiny.

But everyone had gone. He'd missed the end of the play. He'd gone to sleep. Amos would have found the genie bottle in the staffroom. Sure to have done. He'd have gone away without changing him back to his proper size.

How long since the play had ended? How long since the children had filed from the hall?

Without thinking of whether he could still fly or not, Nick threw himself off the curtains and down into the hall. He landed in the middle of the floor. He didn't care now whether anyone saw him or not.

He listened. He heard children in the classrooms. At least school wasn't over. He darted towards the hall doors. Perhaps Amos hadn't gone yet. Nick heard the phone ring and the headmaster's voice.

Had he dreamt after all that Amos had come to the

school and brought his play? He stopped and looked around. What evidence was there? The chalk marks on the floor. He took off again. Just as he was rising in the air a voice called, "Hey! Stop!"

"Mark!" Nick stopped and turned. "I'm in terrible trouble. Listen!" But it wasn't his friend.

The tall figure of Amos leaped from the top of a vaulting box and strode towards him. He towered over Nick.

"Stay where you are!" he commanded. "No more tricks. It won't be the magpie I send after you if you disappear again, my lad. I've just about had enough of you."

"But — !" Nick said. He stepped back in order to see Amos better.

"Where's my genie?" Amos demanded. "I told you *not* to move!"

"I was only — " but Nick wasn't given the chance to finish his sentence.

"The trouble you've caused me!" Amos went on. "Poor Gazza — you've nearly given him a nervous breakdown with your disappearing tricks. And Nushing — I promised her a week's sleep."

"But it wasn't like that!" Nick protested. "I didn't mean to cause any trouble. I just wanted some fun."

"Stay still, I told you!" Amos shouted.

"All I did was find the rotten bottle by the bridge," Nick said, almost in tears. "It wasn't my fault your genie sealed himself in."

"Corked himself?"

"And when I tried to take it out again I was too little

and the bottle rolled in the river."

"River!" Amos suddenly laughed. "I suppose that's what it must seem like to you! Shybad must have been more put out than I thought. Oh no — that means you don't know where he is."

"But I do," Nick said. "He's in the staffroom. Or at least he was. He granted me the wish to fly, though I didn't really want him to. Please, could you turn me back to my normal size as soon as possible?"

"That should be simple enough," Amos said, "once we get our hands on Shybad." He leant and scooped Nick up. "To the staffroom we go. Is it the room I noticed at the end of the corridor past the headmaster's office?" He pushed the hall doors open.

"Genies are lazy creatures," he said. "You've got to have the knack of waking them up properly. If not they can get really obstinate, call black white, swear it's day when it's night. Sit tight if we meet anyone."

"Ah, Mr Amos!" The headmaster rushed out of his office. "It was an absolutely marvellous show. The children and all the staff enjoyed it immensely, by far the best theatrical event this school has ever seen. How about booking you for some time in the future? Christmas, say?" He didn't seem to have noticed Nick sitting in Amos' arms or to realise he had slept through the play.

Amos said, "I promise I'll give you a ring next time I'm in the area. Oh, there's just one thing — "

"Yes?" the headmaster said.

A tremendous scream came from the direction of the staffroom.

The headmaster turned pale.

The scream petered out.

"Don't worry. I'll see what the matter is," Amos said. "I think it's what I'm looking for. Wait here a second."

The door at the far end of the corridor flew open. Mrs Bate burst out and very nearly knocked Amos over.

"Headmaster!" she called. She ran incredibly fast. "That bottle one of the children found in the stream earlier — I couldn't open it when it was brought in, but this time when I pulled the cork flew out and — !" She tugged at the headmaster's arm. *"You go and see!"*

Amos peered round the staffroom door. Nick peered with him. He saw the genie. The genie saw him. A flicker of annoyance passed over its face.

"Ah, Shybad!" Amos said. "Be a good fellow. Get back in that bottle without any of your usual arguments, will you? This is an emergency. No! *No* arguments!" He picked up the cork, pushed it into the top of the bottle, then swiftly went to the window and stepped through the flapping curtains.

15

"I don't know where Shybad learnt that trick," Amos said as they chugged away from the school in his black van. The new big end hadn't made a great deal of difference to the engine. With an important name like that you would have thought it would. "When he's awake and doesn't want to be disturbed he hangs on to the cork. I've never known another genie like him. He's a real handful!"

"How many genies have you got?" Nick asked. "I think you're pretty brave having anything to do with them at all. I mean, I don't even mind handling snakes, but I couldn't have them round me all the time."

Amos turned the van towards the main road.

"How many? It's a job to say." He scratched his head. "They tend to drop in. A couple of dozen, I suppose." Nick gasped. "They're not as bad as they seem," Amos went on. "A few can be a bit awkward at first, but when you get to know their little ways, no problem. They're like humans — a little flattery and patience never does any harm. Turn right?"

Nick stood up on the passenger seat, hanging on to the seat-belt. "If you're taking me home, yes, right and then left a little further on. You are going to turn me

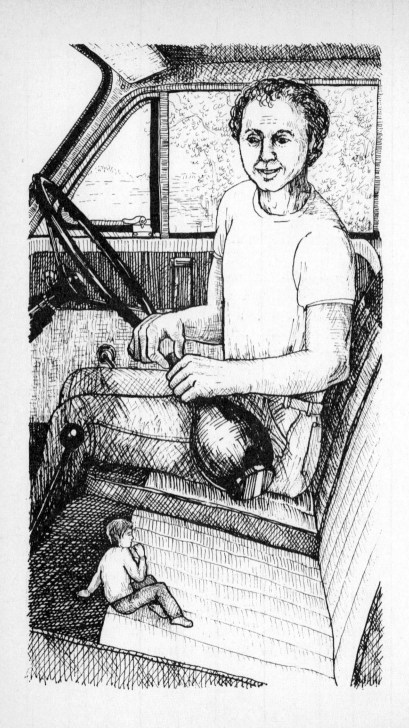

back to normal size first, aren't you?"

"Me?" Amos was amused. "I can't do tricks like that!"

Nick went cold. "Who then?"

"Why, Shybad, of course!" Amos laughed. "You've got three wishes, haven't you? I know you've had two already, but I think Shybad owes you both of them back for having been so awkward. You'll have to use your first wish to turn yourself back to normal size, of course. What will you do with the other two?" He drew into a convenient lay-by and switched off the engine. "Ready?" He drew the cork.

16

Nick lay in bed that night. He was back to his normal size. He wondered what his parents would think in the morning. An envelope containing the first prize of 'Genie's Wonder Game' prize draw would land through the letter box. Had he put enough noughts on the cheque?

And would Mark and his class-mates, Mrs Wright and all the staff at his school remember the day he uncorked Shybad's bottle? His third wish was that everyone should forget what had happened at school today. Perhaps everyone would think it was still Tuesday tomorrow instead of Wednesday. Well, it wouldn't be long before he found out. Would he remember himself?